CHIHUAHUA POWER!

Adapted by Andrea Posner-Sanchez
from the script by Katherine Sandford

Illustrated by Eren Unten

 A GOLDEN BOOK · NEW YORK

TM and © 2015 Paul Frank Industries LLC. Paul Frank and all related logos, characters, names, and distinctive likenesses thereof are the exclusive property of Paul Frank Industries LLC. All rights reserved. Used under authorization. Published in the United States by Golden Books, an imprint of Random House Children's Books, a division of Penguin Random House LLC, 1745 Broadway, New York, NY 10019, and in Canada by Random House of Canada, a division of Penguin Random House Ltd., Toronto. Golden Books, A Golden Book, A Little Golden Book, the G colophon, and the distinctive gold spine are registered trademarks of Penguin Random House LLC.

randomhousekids.com

ISBN 978-0-553-52388-1 (trade) — ISBN 978-0-553-52389-8 (ebook)

Printed in the United States of America

10 9 8 7 6 5 4 3 2 1

Now that Chachi the Chihuahua has moved into The Box, things are even more fun than before! Clancy loves to play basketball with Chachi.

"It's a doggone slam dunk!" shouts Duncan the basketball hoop as Clancy and Chachi make a basket.

Just then, Ping walks over. "Can I play with Chachi now?" she asks. "I need his paws for my art project."

Ping and Chachi head to the arts and crafts area. She has the little pup dip his paws in paint and dance across her picture. Soon she has a new masterpiece!

"This is *paw*-some!" Ping exclaims.

Sheree comes in looking for Chachi.
"Can I play with him now, Ping?" she asks.
"The Wandering Wardrobe and I have
been working on a big surprise."

"It's doggy dress-up day!" announces the Wandering Wardrobe. Chachi jumps inside and is soon dressed as a fire dog . . .

. . . and a clown! Sheree takes pictures of Chachi in lots of different outfits.

Not long after, Worry Bear comes over
and finds the cute dog with a lampshade on
his head.

"Chachi, I've been looking all over for you,"
he says. "It's time to practice your tricks."

With Worry Bear's help,
Chachi can sit up,

roll over,

and even do a backflip!

Meanwhile, Julius Jr. notices a problem
with the door to the Invention Dimension.
"Power level low!" cries Alexander
Graham Doorbell as his bushy mustache
droops lower and lower.

"The Invention Dimension sure uses
a lot of electricity," says Julius Jr.

Julius Jr. hears Chachi barking and Worry Bear laughing. He hurries over to find the little Chihuahua break-dancing!

"Chachi has so much energy," Julius Jr. says. "That gives me an idea for a new invention!"

A short while later, Julius Jr. presents his best invention yet. "The Chacherator measures and captures all of Chachi's doggy energy, turning it into electricity for the Invention Dimension," he explains as he places the invention on Chachi's head. "The more he moves, the more power he creates!"

"Coolio!" yells Clancy.

The friends keep Chachi on the move. He plays more basketball, does more art, poses for more pictures, and practices more tricks.

But now the poor pup is exhausted!
The Chacherator falls off Chachi's head,
and when no one is looking, he crawls
under the coffee table to take a nap.

Julius Jr. shows Worry Bear a
printout from his invention.
    "Chachi's energy level is going down,
down, down," he says. Then they notice
that the Chacherator is on the floor—
and Chachi is nowhere to be found!

Everyone rushes to the Hall of
Doors in hopes of finding Chachi.
When they get to the door to
Icelaska, they hear barking. The
friends put on their warm
hats and go inside.

They find Shaka Brah with his sled dogs, but no Chihuahua.

"Well, it's just after snack time, so if I were you, I'd look under the coffee table," says the yeti. "Chachi likes to nap there after his snack of exactly three organic dog biscuits, one cup of free-range kibble, and water."

"Snack? Water?" asks Sheree.

"Sure, he's always really hungry and thirsty after he comes in from his run," Shaka Brah explains.

The friends realize they haven't been taking good care of Chachi. They thank Shaka Brah for the doggy tips and rush home.

"I'm going to modify the Chacherator so it tracks your food, water, and sleep," Julius Jr. tells Chachi. "That way we won't forget again."

"I'll never forget, now that I know, 'cause I love Chachi!" Ping says, giving Chachi a big hug.

Worry Bear and Sheree bring Chachi
some water and a bowl of food.

After Chachi eats and drinks, Julius Jr. puts the Chacherator back on the little pup's head. Chachi happily barks and runs around. His energy level has gone up, up, up, and the Invention Dimension is full of electricity.

"Now, that's what I call Chihuahua power!" says Alexander Graham Doorbell.